READING RAINBOW®
READERS

FAMILY STORIES

YOU CAN RELATE TO

SeaStar Books

NEW YORK

Special thanks to Amy Cohn, Leigh Ann Jones, Valerie Lewis, and Walter Mayes for the consultation services and invaluable support they provided for the creation of this book.

Reading Rainbow® is a production of GPN/Nebraska ETV and WNED-TV Buffalo and is produced by Lancit Media Entertainment, Ltd., a JuniorNet Company. *Reading Rainbow*® is a registered trademark of GPN/WNED-TV.

The following are gratefully acknowledged for granting permission to reprint the material in this book: "Sloppy Kisses" from *Henry and Mudge in the Family Trees* by Cynthia Rylant, illustrated by Suçie Stevenson. Text copyright © 1997 by Cynthia Rylant. Illustrations copyright © 1997 by Suçie Stevenson. Used by permission of Simon & Schuster Books for Young Readers, an imprint of Simon & Schuster Children's Publishing Division. • "Footprints" from *Lionel and Louise* by Stephen Krensky, illustrated by Susanna Natti. Text copyright © 1992 by Stephen Krensky. Illustrations copyright © 1992 by Susanna Natti. Used by permission of Dial Books for Young Readers, a division of Penguin Putnam Inc. • "Happy Birthday, Mom!" from *Rex and Lilly Family Time* by Laurie Krasny Brown, illustrated by Marc Brown. Copyright © 1995 by Laurie Krasny Brown and Marc Brown. Used by permission of Little, Brown and Company, Inc. • Selections from "Doing Things Pip's Way" from *The Grandma Mix-Up*. Copyright © 1988 by Emily Arnold McCully. Used by permission of HarperCollins Publishers. • "Questions" from *More Tales of Oliver Pig* by Jean Van Leeuwen, illustrated by Arnold Lobel. Text copyright © 1981 by Jean Van Leeuwen. Illustrations copyright © 1981 by Arnold Lobel. Used by permission of Dial Books for Young Readers, a division of Penguin Putnam Inc.

SeaStar Books • A division of North-South Books Inc.

ISBN 1-58717-103-1 (reinforced trade binding) 10 9 8 7 6 5 4 3 2 1
ISBN 1-58717-104-X (paperback edition) 10 9 8 7 6 5 4 3 2 1

CONTENTS

SLOPPY KISSES

BY Cynthia Rylant

PICTURES BY Suçie Stevenson

On the day of the reunion
Henry's family
drove to
Annie's house.

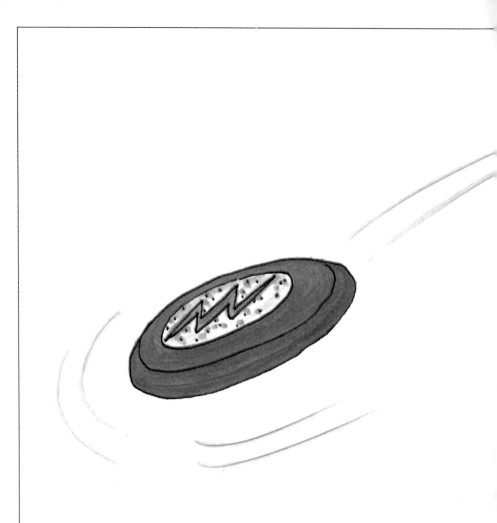

Henry brought a new Frisbee
for Annie,

a tennis ball
for Mudge,

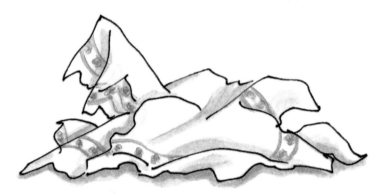

and a paper towel
for himself.
For sloppy kisses.

When they got to Annie's house,
people were everywhere.

In the yard,
on the porch,
all through the house.
And a few were even
in the trees!

Henry suddenly felt nervous.

So many relatives!

What would they say?

Would they be nice?

Would they be friendly?

Would they understand *dog drool*?

Henry and Mudge
got out of the car.

Henry felt very shy.

Suddenly, Annie saw him
from up in a tree.
"Hi Henry!" Annie called.
"Hi Mudge!"

"MUDGE?" a relative
on a swing said.

"MUDGE?" a relative
on the porch said.

"MUDGE?" said somebody
in the house.

"Hey everybody!" shouted
Aunt Sally from another tree.
"It's MUDGE!"

And a million relatives
came running with
a million sloppy kisses—
and all of them for Mudge!
Henry smiled proudly.
Mudge wagged and wagged and wagged.

No one loved a sloppy kiss
better than Mudge.
He was made
for family reunions!

FOOTPRINTS

BY Stephen Krensky

PICTURES BY Susanna Natti

Lionel was sitting in the kitchen
reading a book.
Louise came in holding a jar
of tadpoles.
She slowly climbed the stairs
and put the tadpoles in her room.
"There," she said. "Safe and sound."
When she turned around,
she saw muddy footprints
on the rug.

She followed them down the stairs
and through the hall to the kitchen.
"Lionel," she shouted, "why didn't
you tell me my sneakers were dirty?"
Lionel looked up.
"I wasn't watching," he said.
Louise sighed.

"I'll have to clean this up fast.

Father and Mother will be home soon.

They are just across the street."

She filled a pail with soap and water.

Then she got the mop and the sponge.

Lionel watched her.

He knew how Louise must feel.

It was not a good feeling.

"I'll help you," he said.

"Really?" said Louise.

"Thanks. I'll do the kitchen.

You start in the hall."

Lionel scrubbed the carpet.

The footprints spread into

brown smudges.

Lionel rubbed harder.

The smudges got bigger.

Louise finished in the kitchen.

She came out to see

how Lionel was doing.

"*Arrrgh!*" she screamed.

"Well, I'm not done yet," said Lionel.

"I can see that," said Louise.

She took the sponge from Lionel.

Then she rubbed really hard.

She squeezed the dirty sponge

into the pail again and again.
Lionel got fresh water
from the kitchen three times.
When they finished the last footprint,
Louise let out a deep sigh.

Then she turned around.

"Oh no!" she cried.

"Look at the wall!"

Lionel looked.

His fingerprints were everywhere.

"I'll get more water,"

he said quickly.

"No, no," said Louise.

"Don't move."

She ran for some towels and fresh water.

Then she scrubbed and cleaned

and scrubbed some more.

Lionel held the dirty towels.

Finally she was done.

Louise slumped into a chair.

"Where should I put the towels?"
Lionel asked.

"I'll take them," said Louise.

"Why don't you go out and play?"

"Are you sure?" Lionel asked.

Louise nodded. "I'm sure.

I'm positive!

Thanks for your help, Lionel.

But, please . . . Go!"

"Okay," he said.

He was glad he had helped Louise.

Maybe he would try it more often.

HAPPY BIRTHDAY, MOM!

BY Laurie Krasny Brown

PICTURES BY

Marc Brown

"Surprise, surprise, surprise," said Rex.

"This will be Mom's best birthday!"

"Shh!" said Lilly. "Mom will hear you!"

"This will be the best frosting," said Lilly.
"Yellow!"
"Or blue. I like blue frosting," said Rex.

"Can I help?" asked Mom.
"Please, Mom!" said Rex.
"Don't help! Don't look!"

"What can I draw on Mom's card?"
asked Rex.

"Draw something Mom likes," said Lilly.

Rex tried to think. What does Mom like?

"Can I help?" asked Dad.

"Please, Dad!" said Lilly. "Don't help!"

"This is a surprise."

"Let's set the table," said Lilly.

"Forks here, spoons here."

"Hats here!" said Rex.

"Mom," said Rex and Lilly,
"you can come in now!"

"Oh, my!" said Mom.
"This is my best birthday!
And you did all this with no help!"

"Oh, Mom," said Lilly,
"you can help us now."
"I can?" said Mom.
"You can help us clean up!" said Rex.

DOING THINGS PIP'S WAY

BY Emily Arnold McCully

Pip went outside
to swing high, on the swing.
Grandma Nan wanted
to do things one way,
and Grandma Sal wanted
to do things another way.
Pip wanted to do things
the way Mom and Dad and Pip
always did them.

The grandmas were talking
by the window.
"A child needs rules, Sal,"
said Grandma Nan.
"A child needs fun, Nan,"
said Grandma Sal.

"My rule is bed at 8 o'clock,"
said Grandma Nan.
"Oh, loosen up,"
said Grandma Sal.
"A body gets
the sleep it needs."

"STOP!" cried Pip.
"I do not want
to do everything two ways.
I want to do them our way,
like every day
when Mom and Dad are home."
"How is that, dear?"
asked Grandma Nan.

"I clean my room
once a week.
I make my own lunch
every day.
I don't take a nap
unless I want to,
and I never have candy
in the morning
except at Christmas.
No TV on nice days,
and I can get dirty when I play.
And I don't eat vegetables
all mixed up with meat."

"What do you think, Sal?"
asked Grandma Nan.
"The child has a point,"
said Grandma Sal.

"Pip, we will try
to do things your way,"
said Grandma Nan.
"How do we begin?"

"It is almost my bedtime,"
said Pip.
"But first
I put on my pajamas,
and then I brush my teeth
and pet kitty
and wash my face.
Then I look out for stars
and eat a cookie
and run my trucks,
and then I bounce on my bed
if I feel like it.
Then you can read me a story."

Pip got ready for bed.

The grandmas waited.

Finally

Pip crawled under the covers.

Then Grandma Nan

read the first page,

and Grandma Sal

read the next page

of Pip's bedtime book.

They took turns

to the very end.

QUESTIONS

BY Jean Van Leeuwen

PICTURES BY Arnold Lobel

Father and Oliver
went walking
in the snow.
"Father," said Oliver,
"how many snowflakes are up
in the sky?"
"So many," said Father,
"that no one can count them all."

"I can count to one hundred,"
said Oliver.
"There are even more than that,"
said Father.
"Millions and millions."
Father and Oliver looked down
at the ground.

"Father," said Oliver,
"where did the garden go
when the snow came?"
"It is still there," said Father,
"sleeping under the snow
until spring comes."
"When spring comes,
will my flowers come back?"
asked Oliver.
"Not the same ones," said Father.
"But under the ground
the beginnings of new flowers
are waiting.

When the sun warms the earth,
they will come up."
Father and Oliver looked up
at the trees.
"Father," said Oliver,
"where do the birds go
when it snows?"

"Some fly away to warmer places,"
said Father.
"And some stay in their nests,
where it is snug and warm."
"Is our house like a nest?"
asked Oliver.
"Yes," said Father.
"And now I think it is time for us
to go inside and get snug and warm."

Father and Oliver took off
their snow clothes.
"Father," said Oliver,
"why are my toes still cold?"
"It takes a few minutes for the warm
to get to your toes," said Father.
"But I know what will help."

Father made two cups of hot cocoa.
Then he and Oliver sat
in the big chair next to the fire.
"Father," said Oliver,
"when you were little,
did your father know
just how to warm you up?"

"Yes," said Father.
"He always did."
Father took a book from the shelf.
"Here is a picture of my father
and me when I was little," he said.
"But why does that picture
look just like my father and me?"
asked Oliver.

"Because Grandfather and you and I
are all in the same family,"
said Father.
"Father," said Oliver,
"when you were little, where was I?"
"When I was little,
you had not yet been born,"
said Father.

"It is like the flowers
in our garden waiting for spring.
Everything has a time to grow.
And now, little Oliver,
I have a question for you."
"What is it?" asked Oliver.
"Why do you ask so many questions?"
asked Father.

"I think it is because I want
to know a lot of things,"
said Oliver.
Father hugged Oliver.
"Someday I think you will know
a lot of things," he said.
"Father," said Oliver,
"my toes are warm now."
"I am glad," said Father.